A lbert Le Blanc, the toy polar bear, was happy at Mr Jolly's toy shop. It's true, he didn't actually look happy, but. . . well, that was another story.
And this is a different story. . .

For Harry!
With heaps of love
from Grandpa.
✗ ✗ ✗

First published in Great Britain
by HarperCollins Publishers Ltd in 2007

1 2 3 4 5 6 7 8 9 10

ISBN-13 978-0-00-725925-0   ISBN-10 0-00-725925-5

HarperCollins Children's Books is a division of
HarperCollins Publishers Ltd

Text and illustrations copyright © Nick Butterworth 2007

The author/illustrator asserts the moral right to be
identified as the author/illustrator of this work.

A CIP catalogue record for this title
is available from the British Library.

visit our website at:
www.harpercollinschildrensbooks.co.uk

Printed and bound by Printing Express, Hong Kong

Special thanks to Old Ginger Tom from 'The Whisperer'
for his guest appearance as 'Cat on Shed Roof'

Albert Le Blanc To The Rescue

Nick Butterworth

HarperCollins *Children's Books*

Every day, Albert Le Blanc sat on his shelf waiting for the moment when he might be chosen as a special present for a lucky boy or girl. Yes, he would like that.

His friend, Sally the hippo, had been picked out only a couple of weeks before.

Now, Albert watched out for her each day as she went past the shop. When she did, Sally would wink at Albert and he would give the smallest little wave back.

One wet Wednesday morning, Sally the hippo had an accident.

Right in front of Mr Jolly's shop, she fell with a splash into a large puddle. Then, oh dear, she was trodden on by a great, big, muddy boot!

Poor Sally. Only Albert Le Blanc seemed to notice. He couldn't say anything out loud, but inside, he was shouting, "Help! Somebody please help Sally!"

Somebody had noticed and somebody did help. But it was not the girl who Sally belonged to. It was a lady who picked up Sally.

Albert Le Blanc watched as she squeezed out Sally like a wet sponge and then sneakily popped her into her shopping bag! This was terrible. Sally the hippo was being stolen!

The toys of Mr Jolly's toy shop were shocked.
That evening, after the shop was shut, they did not chatter and play as they usually did. Instead, they worried about what might happen to their friend.

Would Sally be sold to someone else? Would she be given away? Would she be dribbled on by a baby? Used as a cushion? A beanbag? A raffle prize...?

"Please!" said Albert Le Blanc. "This is too much. I just wish she was here."

Suddenly, Jack-in-a-box shouted, "Look everybody!"

From where he was perched on a window sill, Jack could see into the yard of the house next door. There was Sally! It looked like she had been washed and now, dripping wet, she had been pegged out on a washing line to dry.

"Oh! Poor Sally," said Pickle the mouse. "She looks so unhappy."

"It certainly looks like her spirits have been dampened," said Toby the cat.

"But she is here!" said Albert Le Blanc. "And we must rescue her!"

lbert Le Blanc pushed against the window.
It creaked and then swung open.

"Sally! Sally!" he called in a loud whisper.

Sally looked up. "Oh! Hello. . . everyone.

How nice to see you. . ."

"We're going to rescue you," called Albert.

Sally smiled. "How kind," she said.

The trouble was, Sally was a long way down.

How could they reach her?

It seemed impossible. . .

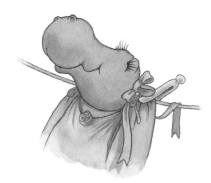

"Can I help, at all?" said a voice. Lofty was a crane. Old and a little bit rusty. It seemed like he had been in the toy shop for ever.

"Of course!" said Albert Le Blanc. "Do your winches work? Is your string still strong?"

"Never better!" said Lofty. The other toys looked at each other.

"Then let us waste no time!" said Albert. "I have an idea..."

Albert Le Blanc's plan was bold and dangerous.

To the sound of worrying clicks and squeaks, Lofty began to lower Albert from the window, down towards his friend, Sally.

The other toys watched nervously.

A sudden hiss from a cat, who had been dozing on a shed roof, startled Albert Le Blanc.

"Don't mind me," said Albert, trying to smile at the cat. "I'm just. . . er. . . hanging around."

Albert Le Blanc was not very good at smiling. He was friendly and brave and he could speak French. But smiling. . . Not really.

The cat looked rather confused and decided that Albert was best left alone.

Click-squeak, click-squeak, click-squeak. . .
Down, down, down, went Albert le Blanc.
Click-squeak-squeeeee. . . CLICK!

Bouncing gently and spinning slowly round,
Albert le Blanc stopped just below Sally.

"Now," said Albert, "climb on to my back."

"I'd love to, dear," said Sally, "but I can't.
I'm pegged."

Albert Le Blanc groaned. What could he do?
If he unpegged Sally, she would fall to the
ground.

A little click-squeak from Lofty told Albert
that he needed to think quickly. But all he
could think of was how thin and frayed Lofty's
string suddenly seemed to be.

"I can help!" called Pickle.
Without waiting to be asked, Pickle
began to climb nimbly down Lofty's string.

As Pickle passed the cat, he half opened
his eyes. Then he slyly licked his lips.

"Don't even think about it, mon ami," said a
growly voice from below. The cat looked down
and stared at Albert. Then, to everyone's relief,
he got up and slunk away.

As quickly as she could, Pickle unpegged Sally from the washing line and Sally fell heavily on to Albert Le Blanc's back.

"Ooof!" groaned Albert.

"Sorry, dear," said Sally. "It's the weight of the water. I'm not quite dry yet."

"Heave-ho, Lofty," said Jack-in-a-box.

Slowly and with one or two scary moments on the way, Albert Le Blanc, Sally and Pickle were winched back up to where the other toys were waiting.

There was a great cheer.

"Hooray for Albert and Lofty!"

"And for Pickle, too!" said Albert. "We must not forget brave Pickle."

Pickle blushed. "And brave Sally, too," she said.

"It must have been horrid being so wet."

"We hippos are used to getting wet," said Sally. "But I don't mind if I never again see the inside of a spin-dryer!"

The next morning, the doorbell of Mr Jolly's toy shop tinkled and into the shop came a little girl called Amy Foster with her mum. Amy looked as if she might have been crying.

"I know, sweetheart," said Amy's mum, "but these things happen. Have a look round. I'm sure you'll see something. . ."

Amy gazed around at all the wonderful toys. It was very hard to choose.

"Him!" said Amy at last, pointing at Albert Le Blanc. "I saw him before. He's so sweet."

"Are you sure?" asked Amy's mum.

"I'm sure," said Amy.

Amy's mum paid Mr Jolly and Albert Le Blanc was put into one of Mr Jolly's special bags.

Suddenly, Amy squealed. "Sally! It's Sally! Oh, Sally, where have you been?"

Mr Jolly was as surprised as Amy. He knew that Amy had bought Sally with her birthday money only two weeks ago. Now, here was Sally, back in his shop. It was a mystery, except, of course, to the toys of Mr Jolly's toy shop.

"I don't understand it," said Mr Jolly, "but you must have Sally back at once."

Amy took Sally and cuddled her. Then she looked at Albert Le Blanc peeping out of his bag.

"Oh, but... but..." said Amy, "do I have to give him back?"

"Well," said Amy's mum, "you do still have some birthday money left..."

Sally the hippo and Albert Le Blanc were carried out of Mr Jolly's toy shop by a very happy Amy Foster.
"Thank you, thank you, thank you," said Amy.
"He's so lovely. I just want to hug him."

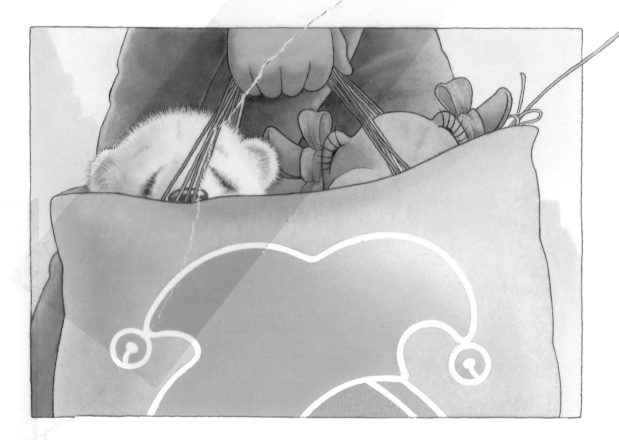

Sally the hippo smiled to herself. "I know just what the girl means," she said.